Barbara Nichol

Safe
and
Sound

Illustrated by

Anja Reichel

Tundra Books

Text copyright © 2003 by Barbara Nichol
Illustrations copyright © 2003 by Anja Reichel

Published in Canada by Tundra Books,
481 University Avenue, Toronto, Ontario M5G 2E9

Published in the United States by Tundra Books of Northern New York,
P.O. Box 1030, Plattsburgh, New York 12901

Library of Congress Control Number: 2003103551

National Library of Canada Cataloguing in Publication

Nichol, Barbara (Barbara Susan Lang)
  Safe and Sound / Barbara Nichol ; illustrated by Anja Reichel.

ISBN 0-88776-633-1

I. Reichel, Anja II. Title.

PS8577.I165S34 2003   jC813'.54   C2003-901517-3
PZ7

We acknowledge the financial support of the Government of Canada through the Book Publishing
Industry Development Program and that of the Government of Ontario through the Ontario
Media Development Corporation's Ontario Book Initiative. We further acknowledge the support
of the Canada Council for the Arts and the Ontario Arts Council for our publishing program.

Design by Kong Njo
Printed and bound in Hong Kong, China

1 2 3 4 5 6   08 07 06 05 04 03

For Linda and Amy McQuaig, two respectable ladies traveling alone.

ACKNOWLEDGMENTS

*Many many thanks, as ever, to Kathy Lowinger,
and to Sue Tate, Kong Njo, and Kathryn Cole.*

In the bookstore there are journals
    of two dogs named Safe and Sound.
Two dogs who sought adventure
    so they went the whole world round.
(Or thought they sought adventure,
    or thought so when at first
They came up with their plan:
    they would succumb to travel thirst.)

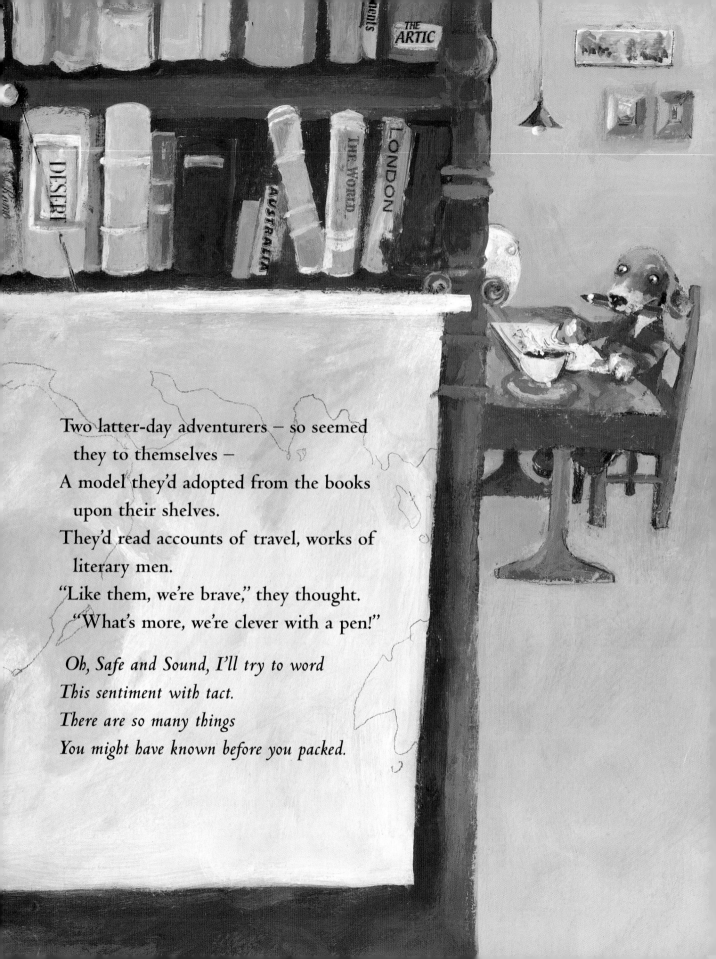

Two latter-day adventurers — so seemed
    they to themselves —
A model they'd adopted from the books
    upon their shelves.
They'd read accounts of travel, works of
    literary men.
"Like them, we're brave," they thought.
    "What's more, we're clever with a pen!"

Oh, Safe and Sound, I'll try to word
This sentiment with tact.
There are so many things
You might have known before you packed.

At the outset of their journey,
　　this is where their woes began.
As soon as they were airborne
　　they commenced to rue their plan.
How had these two not known this,
　　when they made their plans to fly?
The truth they soon discovered
　　is that planes go much too high.

Their first stop was in London. Here they panicked on the bus.
(They found that "all the cars drive on the different side from us.")

And on the boat to France, they had "the closest of close shaves."
On the Channel it was choppy. "No one said there would be waves."

Now, look up in the guidebooks,
Under EUROPE, THINGS TO DO.
You'll see it says to travel in the Alps
To see the view.

"Well," wrote the dogs,
  "please go ahead.
But let us emphasize:
The chairlifts are so scary
That you'll have to
  hide your eyes."

"Of Europe as a whole," they wrote, "feel free to disagree,
But Europe as a continent is not our cup of tea.
The money's funny colors. We are stymied by the phones.
The cinema is tainted with salacious overtones.
Perhaps you'll shop at lunchtime? No! The clerks have gone for naps.
And countries aren't the colors that they seem to be on maps."

Oh, Safe and Sound,
I wish when you'd conceived your travel tome
You'd known the world
(Which is quite nice) is not at all like home.

"In Spain they have their dinner when it should be time for bed.
And go to France for snails to eat, for that's what you'll be fed."

"Be warned as well that when you must pay heed to nature's call,
The toilet paper's scratchy, and the bathroom's down the hall.
And please take note," they wrote, "and any tourist will agree
That everywhere there aren't the proper channels on TV."

We come now to a matter
Somewhat awkward to discuss:
"Foreigners," they wrote,
"Are really not at all like us.
Foreigners are different,
It's the way that they were taught.
They think we're different too
But they are wrong
For we are not."

In Venice, of the boatmen on
   the Grand Canal they wrote:
"Has no one told these fellows
   not to stand up in a boat?"

And on the Côte D'Azur they gave
the locals poor reports.
"They think, it seems, it's quite OK
to swim without your shorts."
What's worse: "We have encountered
from Berlin to Borneo
That Foreigners delight in using
words that we don't know."

Oh, Safe and Sound, dear little friends,
We gather from your books
You're finding out
Adventure's not as easy as it looks.

But onward! Other lands would take their drubbing on the page.
"In India they do not keep their tigers in a cage."

"The Arctic is too cold and we can tell you how we know:
We heard it on the grapevine (and we wisely did not go)."

"But we can guarantee that in Japan they eat with sticks,
That Africa has spiders, South America has ticks.
And though this information has a most unlikely ring:
Australia has autumn when it should be time for spring."

Toward the end, the journals are
   confused and overwrought.
"To tell the truth," they wrote,
   "the world is bigger than we thought."
There is a hasty mention of
   "disaster in Khartoum."
(It seems one day the chambermaid
   forgot to clean their room.)

A note on Turkish markets:
   "You'll avoid them if you're wise."
(A fellow brushed against them
   and did not apologize.)

And high atop their camels in their best safari wear
They scribbled: "Desert people do not know it's rude to stare."

Now, we will never know what brought their travels to an end.
Perhaps upon their camels did the final straw descend.
But briefly put, they'd "seen the world from Guam to Galilee."
"And now," they wrote, "there's just one spot we'd dearly love to see."

Their home: across the ocean, which sped by below the plane.
Home: the destination on their tickets on the train.
Home, whose little station they approached with gladdened hearts.
Home, where they could find their door without the use of charts.
Home, where they soon found themselves benightied in their beds
And where they at long last lay down their dear and weary heads.

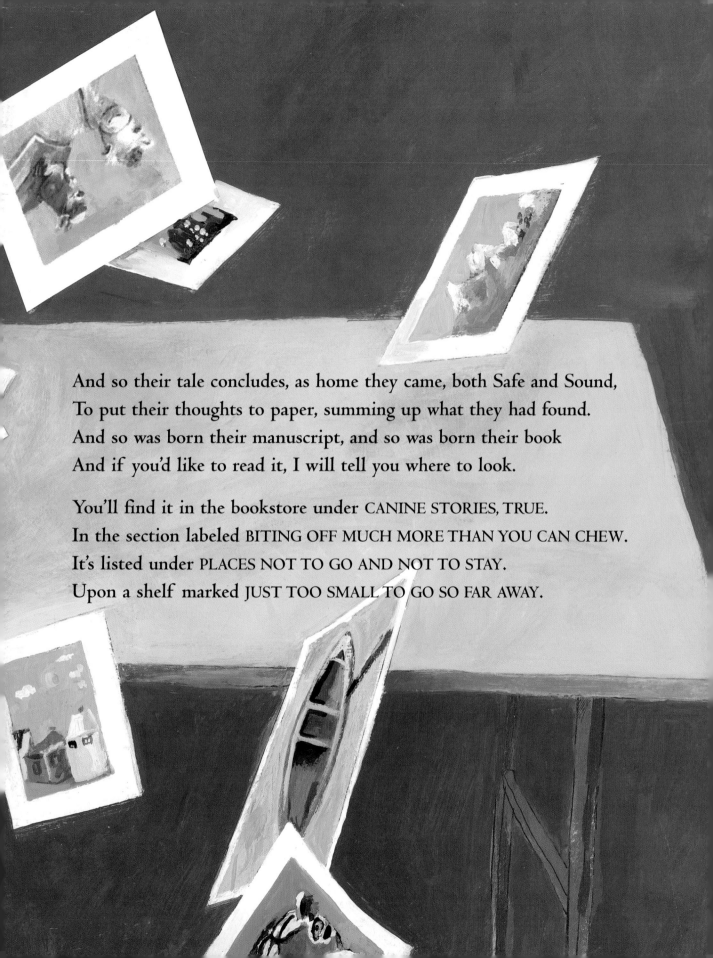

And so their tale concludes, as home they came, both Safe and Sound,
To put their thoughts to paper, summing up what they had found.
And so was born their manuscript, and so was born their book
And if you'd like to read it, I will tell you where to look.

You'll find it in the bookstore under CANINE STORIES, TRUE.
In the section labeled BITING OFF MUCH MORE THAN YOU CAN CHEW.
It's listed under PLACES NOT TO GO AND NOT TO STAY.
Upon a shelf marked JUST TOO SMALL TO GO SO FAR AWAY.

Oh, Safe and Sound, dear homesick souls,
Although you wished to roam,
There's nothing wrong with those who have
A thirst to stay at home.